PRINCESS AILA AND THE UNICORNS

BILL JAMESON

WITH ILLUSTRATIONS BY EMME ROSE

#100/100

To Oprah,
Always Believe!
May the wind always
fill your sails.
♡ Mr. J. Bill Jameson

Hardcover ISBN: 978-1-64438-371-1

Paperback ISBN: 978-1-64438-419-0

Library of Congress Cataloging in Publication Data

Jameson, Bill

Princess Laila and the Unicorns by Bill Jameson

JUVENILE FICTION / Animals / Dragons, Unicorns & Mythical | JUVENILE FICTION / Classics | JUVENILE FICTION / Legends, Myths, Fables / General

Library of Congress Control Number: 2018914455

Printed on Acid Free Paper

Dedicated to Loreley, thank you for the inspiration!

-Mr. J

AILA

is pronounced Eye-lah.

The meaning of Aila is
"from a strong or resilient place."

This meaning paints the picture of a girl that will grow to be a
leader and one that does not back down from a challenge.

Once upon a time when the world was new, there lived a young princess named Aila. She loved animals so much that she learned to speak their languages. She could often be seen whispering to the horses, chatting with the hens, laughing with the lambs, and even giggling with the pigs! She studied all her animals and filled books full of drawings and writings about them.

Aila was the only child of King Fergus of Scotland. The King adored his daughter and the two were very close. As the only heir to his throne, King Fergus knew that someday she would become a great leader.

The forests of Scotland were filled with all sorts of wild animals such as birds, deer, foxes, bears and of course, unicorns.

Aila was always sad when hunters would return from the forests with their kill. Her father explained how important the meat and skins were for his people's survival and reassured Aila that the hunts were done respectfully. Never did the hunters kill young animals or mothers with their young. Aila understood, but still, the killing saddened the little princess.

On one occasion, a hunter returned with a slain unicorn. Aila became enraged and went to her father to argue for a law prohibiting the killing of unicorns. King Fergus told her that his people believed there was powerful magic in the unicorn's horn. The King feared that such a law would make his people so angry they would rebel against the kingdom. "Besides," he would comfort his daughter, "the unicorns are fast and clever! Most escape the hunters."

Aila stared at her father and said, "You are my father and the king. I respect your decision but this argument is not over."

To Aila even one unicorn kill was too many.

She longed for a time when she could learn more about these beautiful creatures. The King, however, would never agree to let her venture so far into the forest alone. Then one day her opportunity came. Her father planned a trip and would be gone for an entire month. Aila would not be watched so closely with King Fergus away from the castle. Now was her chance to find and study the unicorns!

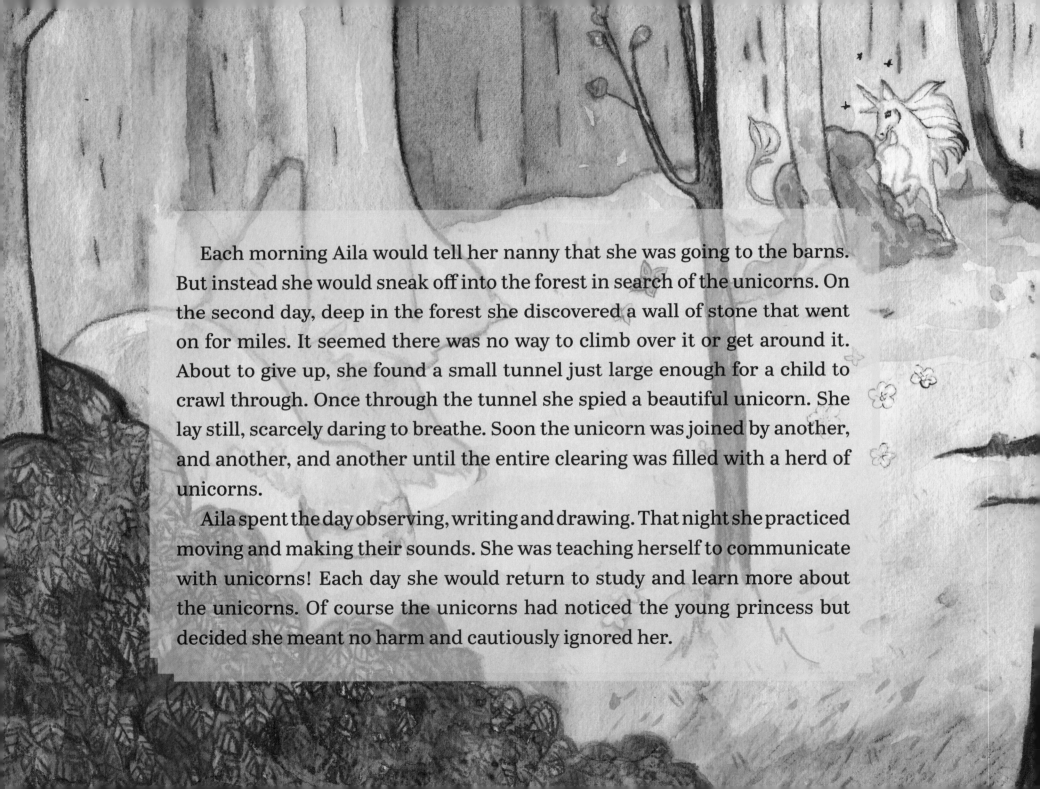

Each morning Aila would tell her nanny that she was going to the barns. But instead she would sneak off into the forest in search of the unicorns. On the second day, deep in the forest she discovered a wall of stone that went on for miles. It seemed there was no way to climb over it or get around it. About to give up, she found a small tunnel just large enough for a child to crawl through. Once through the tunnel she spied a beautiful unicorn. She lay still, scarcely daring to breathe. Soon the unicorn was joined by another, and another, and another until the entire clearing was filled with a herd of unicorns.

Aila spent the day observing, writing and drawing. That night she practiced moving and making their sounds. She was teaching herself to communicate with unicorns! Each day she would return to study and learn more about the unicorns. Of course the unicorns had noticed the young princess but decided she meant no harm and cautiously ignored her.

On the day before her father's return, Aila decided she must speak to the unicorns. Watching and waiting, she noticed an energy of excitement rippling through the herd. Suddenly a large unicorn came out of the forest. All the unicorns bowed their heads in respect. Aila thought this unicorn must be their king. Bravely she stood up, walked softly toward him and curtseyed in respect. She made the soft cooing sound unicorns make when they greet each other. The large unicorn bowed his head and cooed back. Looking at this young girl he instantly realized that she must be a princess.

He crouched low and swung his head toward his tail. Aila climbed on his back. She held on to his mane as he stood up and after a few steps he unfurled his hidden wings. With one leap the pair was flying through the air. They flew above the treetops and over the mountains. He showed Aila the secret place where the unicorns would return at night to be safe. After landing back in the clearing, Aila slipped off his back and thanked him. She promised to return the next day with a gift.

That night King Fergus returned. Aila never had, and never would keep any secrets from her father. She told him all about her visits with the unicorns.

The king was silent for what seemed like an eternity and then he spoke. "My child, I fear for you the most, but also for your unicorns. You see if the hunters learn that you know where unicorns live they will come after you. Some hunters may get greedy and kill them all. I forbid you to visit the unicorns and you must never speak of this again."

Aila paused, collected her thoughts and bravely spoke, "Father you have taught me I must always keep my promises, and I promised the unicorn king a gift. Are you now saying I should break my promise?" "Very well," said the king, "but be careful, and this is your last visit."

Before dawn, Aila snuck out of the castle and followed the shadows into the forest. Clutched in her hand was a satchel with 100 golden beads. When the unicorns came into the clearing, she walked up to the unicorn king and showed him the beads. She then braided one of the beads into his mane. He seemed pleased, so she braided another and another until all 100 beads were braided into his mane.

The king of unicorns pranced around the clearing and his golden beads sparkled in the sun. Then he turned to the princess and signaled for her to have one more ride.

As the pair soared above the trees, the sun reflected on the golden beads, creating a shimmering glow in the sky. The light caught the eye of a hunter, and he loosed an arrow straight at the heart of the unicorn king. Aila saw what was happening, and swung her own body in harm's way. As the arrow struck her leg, Aila screamed and fell toward the earth. Diving below her the unicorn king caught her and flew her back to safety.

The unicorn king knew that the little princess would die without human help. He feared that approaching the human castle would lead to his own death. His love for little Aila, however, was greater than the fear for his own life. He flew her to the castle, over the wall and landed in the courtyard.

People ran screaming and hunters grabbed their bows. But when they saw the princess they called for the king.

When King Fergus arrived, he lifted his daughter from the unicorn's back.

Aila whispered, "He is also a king, please take care of him," and then she fainted.

It was a week before Aila awoke. The healers were able to remove the arrow and heal her wound. She had lost a lot of blood, but she would live.

Her first words to her father were, "Where is the king of the unicorns?" Her father hugged his daughter and whispered, "he is safe, hidden with my personal horses." Aila cried and thanked her father who told her to rest, they would discuss what to do the next day.

In the morning the king came to Aila. He explained to the princess that no unicorn was safe. Aila begged her father to take her to Myron the Sorcerer. "Surely, Myron will know what to do!" the little princess cried.

The sorcerer listened carefully to the story. Myron closed his eyes and after several minutes he spoke. "There is another world where they will be safe. I can create a door to this world. You must tell all the unicorns to pass through this door." Aila smiled and agreed.

"We shall put the door in a secret place so that I should be able to visit them," she said.

"No no my dear princess," Myron spoke. "Once the last unicorn passes through the door we must destroy the door or they will never be safe."

Aila realized this was true, and now it was up to her to keep the unicorns safe. She looked at Myron and spoke, "Tomorrow we shall create the door and I will gather the unicorns and tell them what to do." King Fergus smiled at his daughter and marveled at how she could become so wise at such a young age.

The next day Aila, the King, and the sorcerer gathered in the forest. Aila explained to her unicorn friends what was to happen.

Myron created the doorway to the new world and one by one, each unicorn galloped through the door. Before the king of unicorns passed through the door, he paused and bowed before the princess. She threw her arms around the majestic creature and kissed him goodbye. After the king of unicorns passed through the door, Myron spoke his magic and the door disappeared. The unicorns were safe.

With tears running down her cheeks Aila hugged her father and said, "I have learned that tears can be sad and happy at the same time. I have also learned that sometimes we have to let the things we love go free." King Fergus hugged his daughter and said, "Your mother would be so proud of you, come, let us return to the castle."

On the way home the king spoke, "From this day forward,
people will always wonder what happened to the unicorns of Scotland."
"Someday the story will be told," said Aila, "for this is not The End,
it is but The Beginning."

ABOUT THE AUTHOR

Known as "Mr. J" to his students, Bill Jameson still owns his first hardcover children's book, a Christmas gift from his parents in 1959. Growing up immersed in great literature and storytelling from both parents, becoming a storyteller was inevitable.

Mr. J has been in and out of the classroom telling stories for over 40 years. Princess Aila and the Unicorns is his first book, but a sequel is in progress, as well as more books to come. He has a home in Newfoundland and loves to travel, and of course tell stories! He can be reached at www.storieswithmrj.com.

ABOUT THE ILLUSTRATOR

Emme Rose was born between postings, grew up in the desert, then attended OCADu in Toronto for illustration and graphic design. While her work has been published academically, Princess Aila and the Unicorns is her children's book debut. You can find more of her work on social media under @ emmesketch or at EmmeIllustrates.com!

CPSIA information can be obtained at www.ICGtesting.com
Printed in the USA
BVIW122307190219
540123BV00001B/1